SHARING MY STUNNING HOT WIFE

WIFE SHARING HOTWIFE EROTICA COLLECTION

WIFE SHARING FANTASIES
BOOK THREE

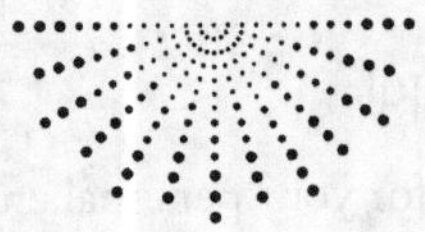

LEE RILEY

Disclaimer

This work of fiction is intended for mature audiences only. It contains sex acts between consenting adults, and characters represented within are eighteen years of age or older. Names, characters, places, and incidents are either the product of the author's imagination or are used fictitiously, and any resemblance to actual persons, living or dead, business establishments, events, or locales is entirely coincidental.

❀ Created with Vellum

ABOUT THIS BOOK

The year is 1963. The music is groovy, the cocktails are strong, and the wives are submissive and obedient. Or, if they aren't, at least the man of the house can train them up with the help of a few of his buddies.

SHARING MY BRIDE WITH MY BOSS

Andrew is an ambitious young gun at the office but he has to prove to his boss Mr. Lloyd that he's got the dominant streak it takes to lead an entire office of his own. What better way to show the older man that he has SOMETHING than to share his untouched bride Caroline. Caroline is in for a few hard lessons that will leave her and both men begging for more.

MY WIFE PAYS MY DEBTS

It's Ricky's turn to host his buddies' weekly poker night and he can't seem to catch a break. He loses hand after hand until he finds himself dipping into his vacation fund. The dominant daddy has a better idea… why not share his hotwife Felicia with the guys? Felicia can submit to this entire group of men.

SHARING MY BRIDE WITH MY BOSS

"No," Andrew shook his head as his pretty wife Caroline laid out a simple beige set of panties along with a matching bra. "Put on the white one."

"Oh!" Caroline paused. "You mean with the lace?" It was what she had come to consider her 'special occasion' set, the one she wore whenever Andrew took her out on a date and expected to make love later in the evening. But she wasn't entirely surprised. Having Andrew's boss Mr. Lloyd over for supper was a special occasion, she guessed. It made sense that Andrew would want his young wife looking and feeling her best, even though Mr. Lloyd would never see the trouble she went to.

"Yeah," Andrew nodded. "That's the one."

Caroline reached for the white lacy garments and slipped them off of the hanger.

"And don't bother with the pantyhose," Andrew continued, "and be sure to wear that blue dress I like."

Caroline didn't respond. She simply took the lingerie into the bathroom, closed the door behind her, and began to undress.

She could hear Andrew out in the living room, fidgeting with the table settings and the cutlery, and she could imagine how nervous he was. He wanted so much to please Mr. Lloyd, to make a good impression. After all, he had only been working at Lloyd, Thompson & Associates for two months. Caroline was just as nervous, although probably not for the same reasons as Andrew.

The thought of Mr. Lloyd sitting at their dining room table, eating with her and her husband made Caroline's stomach flutter. She had never met him but Andrew spoke of him often enough. And he had shown her Mr. Lloyd's photograph, the one taken at last year's Christmas party. "That's him, there," Andrew had said. He had pointed to a distinguished looking man of about forty.

"Oh, he's handsome," Caroline had replied, "in an older sort of way." He looked a bit like Clark Gable, with his thin mustache and wavy brown hair.

Mr. Lloyd had smiled at the camera. His teeth were white and perfect, Caroline remembered, and the top row was full, yet not too large for his mouth. It gave him a charming, boyish sort of look. And his eyes, even in the picture, seemed to sparkle with mischief.

Andrew hadn't been amused by his wife's assessment. "He's more than handsome," he had explained. "He's powerful. He's rich. He's a success."

Caroline knew Andrew envied the man. He was everything her husband wanted to be.

In the picture, Mr. Lloyd had stood next to a woman Caroline supposed was his wife. She had been very pretty in her own right, with shoulder length blonde hair and a tight fitting dress that showed off her curves. Caroline wondered if Andrew had ever seen her in the flesh, or whether she had just been part of the photograph. But it was Mr. Lloyd that Caroline couldn't stop thinking about.

She finished applying her make-up and then stepped into her dress. It was a simple sleeveless affair with a fitted bodice. It had a modest neckline that showed just the barest hint of cleavage, but with the lacy white push-up bra underneath it Caroline felt almost indecently exposed. She slipped on the matching pair of white heels that Andrew had left for her on the bathroom mat and then, after one last look in the mirror, stepped back into the living room.

"Well, what do you think?" She did a little twirl to show off her dress.

Andrew glanced up from his newspaper. "Turn around," he ordered her.

Caroline obeyed immediately, her cheeks blushing at the thought of her husband inspecting her like a prize filly. They had only been married for six months and she was still getting used to the physical aspect of their relationship. The way he spoke to her sometimes made her feel embarrassed. But she had to admit that she liked it as well, the way he treated her. The way he ordered her around. She could never say no to him.

"Mmm..." Andrew grunted, "that's just right."

"Thank you," Caroline smiled and batted her eyelashes.

"You look very pretty," Andrew said. "Mr. Lloyd is going to like what he sees, I think."

Caroline's heart began to beat faster at the thought of Mr. Lloyd's eyes on her. Would he really notice her, even with his beautiful wife around?

"Now, make sure you have everything ready. He should be here any minute."

Caroline nodded and turned to the kitchen. She finished setting the table, making sure the cutlery was just so. Then she put the food on to warm and went to the front door to check her reflection in the hall mirror. Her lipstick was perfect. Her hair was in place. She was ready.

She heard the knock at the door and immediately went to answer it.

Mr. Lloyd was there, a bouquet of flowers in his hand. Caroline was surprised to see that he was alone, though. She had expected him to arrive with his wife.

"Mr. Lloyd!" Caroline held out her hand in greeting. "Welcome to our home."

"Good evening," Mr. Lloyd shook her hand and then handed her the flowers. "I hope you like roses," he said.

"Oh yes!" Caroline took them. "They're my favorite!" She breathed in their scent and then stepped aside to let her guest into the house. "Here," she held out her hand. "Let me take your coat."

Mr. Lloyd handed her his coat and then Caroline led him into the living room, where Andrew greeted him.

"Ah, Mr. Lloyd!" Andrew slapped his boss on the back in an over-familiar manner that Caroline thought looked rather ridiculous. "Welcome, welcome!"

"Hello, Andrew," Mr. Lloyd nodded to his employee and then turned back to Caroline. "So, Andrew tells me you're a new bride."

"Yes," Caroline nodded and smiled as she laid the flowers on the dining room table. "We've only been married since May."

"And how are you liking married life, Mrs. Wright?" Mr. Lloyd asked her.

"It's wonderful, thank you," Caroline answered. "I feel so lucky to have found Andrew."

"Lucky?" Mr. Lloyd raised his eyebrows. "I'm not so sure about that. It's more like Andrew's the one who got lucky." He glanced around the living room in an appraising sort of way. "You've got yourself a pretty wife, Andrew," he continued. "And she's got a good set of tits on her, if you don't mind me saying."

Caroline froze as Mr. Lloyd stared at her breasts. It made her feel self-conscious, but she didn't know what to do except stand there and let him look at her.

"Yes, sir," Andrew answered. "Wait until you see her ass. You're going to love it."

Caroline gasped aloud. She knew that men talked about women in certain ways. But she never would have guessed that her own husband was one of those men. It shocked her to hear him say such things in front of Mr. Lloyd.

"Is that so?" Mr. Lloyd stepped closer to Caroline and put his hand on her shoulder. He squeezed it firmly. "Are you proud of your wife's tits, Andrew?" he asked.

"Yes, sir," Andrew answered. "I'm very proud of them."

"And why is that?" Mr. Lloyd asked.

"Well...they're big, and round, and soft," Andrew answered, as if he were reading from a script. "They fill my hands up nicely."

"That's good," Mr. Lloyd said. "That's very good, Andrew. Tell me...have you and Caroline been together for a long time?"

"Since college," Andrew answered. "We met in our junior year and got married right after we graduated."

"Well, that's very nice," Mr. Lloyd said. "And how old are you, Caroline?"

"Twenty-one, sir," Caroline said.

"Oh my." Mr. Lloyd seemed surprised. "So, you and Andrew have been having sex for a while now, is that right?"

"Sir..." Caroline mewled. Her cheeks were bright red and she hoped neither of the men could tell how embarrassed she was.

"She made me wait for the wedding night," Andrew answered for her. "She's a good girl. Bit of a slow learner, if you know what I mean."

"Oh, I know exactly what you mean," Mr. Lloyd chuckled. "A virgin, then?"

"Oh yes," Andrew nodded.

"And you popped her cherry on your wedding night?"

"Yes, sir," Andrew nodded. "She fussed a little bit but overall she was a good girl about it."

"That's good." Mr. Lloyd slid his hand down Caroline's arm and gave her ass a quick pat. "A good wife should always do as she's told," he said.

Caroline jumped at the contact. She felt humiliated and didn't know what to do. "Excuse me," she finally said and headed towards the kitchen. "I think I hear the oven timer go off."

"Take your time," Mr. Lloyd called after her. "I think Andrew and I would like to talk alone for a few minutes."

Caroline fled into the kitchen. She didn't know what was going on but she knew it had something to do with her. She couldn't believe Andrew was telling Mr. Lloyd such things about her. How could he talk about their private life so casually, and in front of a virtual stranger?

She took the pot roast out of the oven and began to carve it. Then she placed it on a platter and went back into the dining room. She saw that the two men were seated next to each other at the table, and that there was an empty seat across from them. She assumed it was where she was supposed to sit.

"Here we go," Caroline said as she brought the roast to the table. "I hope you like pot roast."

"Mrs. Wright," Mr. Lloyd said. "You and your roast look positively radiant this evening. Absolutely lovely."

Caroline blushed at the compliment.

"Now, sit down." Mr. Lloyd patted the empty chair.

Dinner proceeded relatively as normal, which was a great relief to Caroline. The men talked about work and Mr. Lloyd praised her cooking. The wine flowed and by the time she served dessert, she was feeling much more relaxed.

"What say we move into the living room for a little brandy?" Andrew suggested once Caroline had cleared the table.

"Excellent idea," Mr. Lloyd nodded.

Andrew went into the kitchen and returned with a tray of snifters and a bottle of brandy. He handed one to Mr. Lloyd and then another to Caroline. She sipped hers slowly as the two men talked. It was rich and sweet on her tongue, and it made her feel warm inside.

"So, Caroline," Mr. Lloyd said after a while. "Tell me what you do all day while Andrew's away at work."

"Oh...well, I clean, and do the laundry, and cook, and run errands," Caroline answered.

"And is that enough to keep you busy?" Mr. Lloyd asked.

"Sometimes," Caroline said. "But sometimes it gets a bit lonely."

"I see," Mr. Lloyd nodded. "And what do you do to alleviate that loneliness?"

"Well," Caroline glanced over at Andrew. He was staring at her intently. "I read a lot. And I listen to the radio, or the record player."

"Do you ever touch yourself when you're alone, Caroline?" Mr. Lloyd asked her.

Caroline gasped at his question. "Sir!" she cried, and then she covered her mouth in shock.

"Come now, Caroline," Mr. Lloyd said. "We're all adults here, aren't we? Now, answer the question."

"I..." Caroline looked down at her lap. "No, sir," she answered. "I've never touched myself."

"Why not?" Mr. Lloyd asked her. "Is it because you don't know how?"

Caroline didn't want to answer. She didn't think it was right to talk about such things.

"Answer him, Caroline," Andrew said.

"It's alright," Mr. Lloyd said. "She's shy. We should teach her, so that she doesn't end up getting so lonely that someone takes advantage of her, like the milkman or a traveling salesman. Would you like that, Caroline? Would you like Andrew and I to teach you how to touch yourself?"

Caroline felt like she was going to cry. "Please," she said. "Please, I don't..."

"Don't what?" Mr. Lloyd asked. "Don't understand?" He looked at Andrew. "Andrew, I think your wife is confused."

"Then it's a good thing I've got such a smart boss," Andrew said. "He'll be able to help her, I'm sure."

"Oh, I intend to," Mr. Lloyd nodded. "And Andrew, I think it would be best if we did it together. Show her how it's done. That way she won't be tempted to stray from you."

"I agree," Andrew nodded. "I agree entirely."

"But...but..." Caroline didn't know what to say.

"Caroline." Andrew stared at her sternly. "Come here."

Caroline hesitated but only for a second. She got up and walked over to her husband.

"Sit," Andrew ordered her.

Caroline sat down in Andrew's lap.

"Now," Andrew said. "Mr. Lloyd's going to show you how to touch yourself."

"Andrew!" Caroline cried out. "I...I can't..."

"You will," Andrew insisted. "Mr. Lloyd and I are going to teach you. Now, do as he says."

"Andrew," Caroline mewled.

"Caroline, either you do as you're told or you're going to get a spanking," Andrew threatened her. "Now, be a good girl and do what Mr. Lloyd tells you to do."

Caroline sighed heavily. "Alright," she relented.

"Good," Mr. Lloyd smiled. "Now, Caroline, why don't you start by unbuttoning that dress."

Caroline reached up to the top of her dress and began to slowly undo the buttons. She didn't know why she was doing it. But she was too afraid of what would happen if she didn't.

"That's it," Mr. Lloyd encouraged her. "And when you're finished, take it off and hang it up. You're not going to need it for a while."

Caroline stood up and continued to undress. She was embarrassed to be exposing herself like this but at the same time she could feel the wetness between her legs. She didn't know what was happening to her.

When she was stripped down to her underwear and garters, she hung her dress on the back of a chair and then stood there, waiting for further instructions.

"That's very good," Mr. Lloyd nodded approvingly. "Now, why don't you come over here and sit down?"

Caroline sat down in the empty chair next to Mr. Lloyd. He reached out and ran his fingers along the inside of her thigh. She trembled at his touch.

"Andrew," Mr. Lloyd turned to her husband. "Why don't you come over here and give your wife some encouragement."

Andrew stood up and walked over to Caroline. He knelt down beside her and put his hand on her knee.

"Caroline," he said softly. "We're only trying to help you. We're only trying to show you how to make yourself feel good."

"I...I understand," Caroline whispered. She closed her eyes as Mr. Lloyd slid his hand up to her panties.

"That's it," he whispered. "Just relax."

"What do you think?" Andrew asked Mr. Lloyd.

"I think she's ready," Mr. Lloyd nodded. "It's time we showed her what to do."

"Right," Andrew agreed. He slid his hand up to Caroline's garters and began to roll them down her legs. She shuddered at his touch.

Mr. Lloyd slipped his fingers under the edge of Caroline's panties and tugged them down. She lifted her hips slightly and then gasped as the cool air hit her most intimate place.

"There we go," Mr. Lloyd smiled. "Now, let's show you how to touch yourself."

Caroline felt Mr. Lloyd's fingers glide over her moist lips. She couldn't believe how good it felt. She had never touched herself there before.

"That's it," Mr. Lloyd whispered. "Just relax and let us show you."

"Ohhhh..." Caroline moaned. She could feel her whole body start to tremble.

Mr. Lloyd stroked her gently, sliding his fingers up and down her wet slit. Then he began to tease her clitoris, rubbing it lightly. She gasped and arched her back.

"That's it," Mr. Lloyd whispered. "Now, it's your turn."

Caroline froze in shock. She couldn't believe that Mr. Lloyd was actually telling her to touch herself. But when she glanced over at Andrew he simply nodded.

"Go ahead," he whispered.

"Andrew..." Caroline whimpered.

"Looks like your wife doesn't respect you, my boy," Mr. Lloyd shook his head. "I don't know how you can expect to run an entire office when you can't even get your own wife to obey. Maybe you should spank her."

"Yes, sir," Andrew said. "I think you're right."

"But..." Caroline protested. She didn't want Andrew to spank her. Not in front of Mr. Lloyd.

"Caroline, I've told you before, I don't like it when you talk back to me," Andrew scolded her. "Now, come here and bend over my knee. Or do you want me to take off my belt? Because I will if you don't obey."

Caroline hung her head in shame as she walked over to Andrew. She bent over his knee and closed her eyes.

Andrew raised his hand and brought it down hard on her ass. She yelped in pain.

"That's it," Mr. Lloyd said. "Show your wife what happens when girls talk back to their husbands. She needs to learn now, or else she'll turn into a harpy, you mark my words. A woman has to know who's in charge. And that's her husband. Isn't that right, Andrew?"

"Yes, sir," Andrew nodded. "That's right."

Andrew raised his hand and brought it down on Caroline's ass once more. She cried out in pain but didn't struggle. She knew that if she did it would only make things worse for her.

"Why don't you take those panties off of her," Mr. Lloyd suggested. "Then we can see how red her ass is getting."

Andrew tugged at the waistband of Caroline's panties and pulled them down over her hips. She blushed furiously as he exposed her bare bottom.

"Oh, yes," Mr. Lloyd smiled. "You were absolutely right about her. She does have a great ass."

"Thank you, sir," Andrew said.

"I'm sure it's going to look even better when it's nice and red."

Andrew spanked Caroline again, making her cry out in pain.

"I think she's learned her lesson," Mr. Lloyd said. "Why don't you show her how to touch herself?"

"Yes, sir." Andrew ran his hand over Caroline's bottom. "Are you ready to touch yourself for us, Caroline?" he asked her.

Caroline nodded. She didn't know how to respond.

"Good girl," Andrew said. He reached down and took her hand. "Now, just relax and let me show you."

Andrew guided Caroline's hand between her legs. She could feel how wet she was. How slick and slippery her skin was.

"That's it," Andrew encouraged her. "Just like that."

Caroline began to stroke herself, moving her fingers up and down her lips. It felt so good.

"Do you like that?" Andrew asked her.

"Yes..." Caroline moaned.

"Would you like me to show you something else?" Andrew asked.

"Yes..." Caroline whimpered.

"Andrew, I think you should spank her again," Mr. Lloyd suggested. "And while you're doing that, why don't I show her how to make herself come?"

"Yes, sir," Andrew said. "I think that's a great idea."

Andrew lifted his hand and brought it down hard on Caroline's ass. She cried out in pain.

Mr. Lloyd reached between Caroline's legs and began to stroke her. His fingers felt so much better than hers did.

"Ohhhhh..." Caroline moaned.

"That's it," Mr. Lloyd whispered. "Just relax and let me show you how to make yourself come."

Andrew spanked Caroline again and again as Mr. Lloyd rubbed her. She could feel her body start to tremble. Her whole world seemed to be spinning out of control.

"That's it," Mr. Lloyd whispered. "Come for me, Caroline. Come for me."

Caroline closed her eyes and threw her head back. She had never felt anything so intense. Her whole body seemed to be on fire. She felt like she was flying.

"That's it," Mr. Lloyd whispered. "Just let it go. Just let it happen."

Andrew raised his hand and brought it down on Caroline's ass one last time. She cried out in pain and pleasure. Then her body began to shake uncontrollably. She felt like she was going to explode.

"That's it," Mr. Lloyd whispered. "Let it go. Let it happen. Just let it happen."

Caroline felt her whole body begin to shake. She felt like she was going to die. She couldn't breathe. She couldn't think. She couldn't do anything except let the pleasure consume her.

"That's it," Mr. Lloyd whispered. "Just let it happen. Just let it happen."

Caroline's whole world seemed to explode. She felt like she was floating on air. She had never felt anything so intense. She felt like she was going to die.

"Will you look at that," Mr. Lloyd admired the little show Caroline was putting on. "She loves it. What do you say we teach her a few more tricks tonight, Andrew? Teach her how to suck a man's cock, for starters."

"I think that's a great idea," Andrew said. "But I'll let you start with her, sir. You're our guest, after all."

"Wonderful," Mr. Lloyd said. "Now, Caroline. On your knees. You're going to learn how to suck a man's cock."

"But, sir..." Caroline whispered.

"Looks like she's still resisting," Mr. Lloyd shook his head. "She's a stubborn one! Good thing she's so pretty." He turned to Andrew. "I think she needs some hard lessons tonight, don't you?"

"Yes, sir," Andrew agreed. "I think you're right."

Andrew grabbed Caroline by the arm and pulled her to his side. "Mr. Lloyd is going to teach you how to suck his cock, Caroline," he said. "And I want you to pay attention."

Caroline looked up at him in shock. "Andrew!" she gasped.

"You're going to do what Mr. Lloyd says, Caroline," Andrew told her. "You're going to suck his cock. And you're going to do a good job. Or else."

"Andrew!" Caroline cried. "I...I can't!"

"You will," Andrew insisted. "Now, be a good girl and do as you're told."

Andrew let go of Caroline and she fell to her knees.

"That's better," Mr. Lloyd nodded approvingly. "Now, why don't you take my cock out and give it a nice little kiss?"

Caroline reached up and undid Mr. Lloyd's trousers. She pulled out his cock and then pressed her lips gingerly against it. It was thick and heavy and red and it smelled like sweat and musk.

"Mmm...that's it," Mr. Lloyd moaned. "Now, why don't you give it a little lick?"

Caroline licked the tip of Mr. Lloyd's cock, tasting the salty sweat. She had never done anything like this before and it made her feel ashamed.

"That's it," Mr. Lloyd whispered. "Just like that. Now, take it in your mouth."

Caroline parted her lips and took the very tip of Mr. Lloyd's cock inside, running her tongue over the head.

"Oh yes," Mr. Lloyd moaned. "Just like that. Now, suck on it."

Caroline began to suck on Mr. Lloyd's cock, and he responded by pistoning it gently in and out of her mouth. She could feel it growing even harder as she sucked on it.

"That's it," Mr. Lloyd whispered. "Just like that. Keep sucking. You're doing a very good job, Caroline. Now, why don't you put your hand on my balls and give them a little squeeze?"

Caroline reached up and cupped Mr. Lloyd's balls in her hand. They were heavy and swollen with his seed. She gave them a little squeeze and he groaned in pleasure.

"That's it," Mr. Lloyd moaned. "Keep doing that. Now, take my cock in your mouth and suck on it hard. Take it deeper in your throat. Deeper. Deeper."

Caroline felt Mr. Lloyd's cock touch the back of her throat and she gagged slightly. She tried to pull away but he grabbed the back of her head and held her in place.

"That's it," he whispered. "Just like that. You're a natural born cocksucker, Caroline. Now, keep sucking on it."

Caroline sucked on Mr. Lloyd's cock for what felt like an eternity. He pushed her head down onto his cock, making her take him deep in her throat. She felt like she was going to choke but she didn't dare try to pull away. Finally, after what seemed like forever, he pulled her mouth off of his cock and began to stroke himself.

"Not bad," he grunted. "How about you give your poor husband a turn? Do your wifely duty?"

Caroline glanced over at Andrew, who was staring at her with a look of pure lust on his face. She was shocked at how much he seemed to enjoy watching her suck Mr. Lloyd's cock. He already had his own cock in his hand and he was stroking it as he watched her.

"You heard the man," Andrew said. "Come here and suck my cock."

Caroline crawled over to Andrew and took his cock in her mouth. He was already rock hard and he pushed her head down onto his cock, making her take him deep in her throat. She could taste his precum on her tongue and it made her feel strangely aroused.

"Mmm...that's it," he moaned. "You like sucking on your husband's cock, don't you?"

"Mmm-hmm," Caroline moaned. She could feel her pussy getting wet again.

"That's a good girl," he whispered. "Now, take it deeper. I want to feel my cock hitting the back of your throat."

Caroline took Andrew's cock deeper in her throat, gagging slightly as it touched the back. She felt her pussy growing wetter and wetter as she sucked on his cock.

"Look at that," Mr. Lloyd exclaimed. "She seems to be a natural! A perfect little cocksucker."

"Yes, sir," Andrew moaned. "She's very good at it."

"I'll say," Mr. Lloyd said. "She's soaking wet. Look at this," he dragged a finger up Caroline's lips and showed it to Andrew. "Her pussy is dripping."

"Mmm..." Andrew moaned. "Why don't you show her how a real man fucks a woman, Mr. Lloyd? Give her a proper lesson."

"What a splendid idea," Mr. Lloyd agreed. "And you can watch her while I'm fucking her. See if she learns anything from the lesson."

"Perfect," Andrew nodded. He let go of Caroline's head and she pulled her mouth off of his cock.

"Andrew!" Caroline protested.

"Would you prefer I take you in the ass?" Mr. Lloyd offered. "Is that what you want? For me to stick my cock in your tight little asshole?"

"No!" Caroline cried. "Please!"

"I think that would be a splendid idea," Andrew answered for her. "That way we won't end up with any little Lloyd bastards running around here."

"True, true," Mr. Lloyd chuckled. "Very well, then. I'll take her ass."

"No!" Caroline begged. "I don't understand how..."

"On all fours, Caroline," Andrew ordered her.

"But..." Caroline whimpered.

"Caroline," Andrew said sternly. "Do as you're told. You're not going to get out of this so easily. Now spread your ass open wide for Mr. Lloyd. He's already been so kind to you, teaching you how to suck cock like that. You wouldn't want to be rude to him now, would you?"

Caroline got down on her hands and knees and spread her ass cheeks apart with her fingers. She could feel the cool air on her most private place and it made her blush in shame.

Mr. Lloyd knelt down behind her and began to stroke his cock.

"Andrew..." Caroline whispered. "Andrew, please..."

"Shhh..." Andrew held his wife by the hair. "Just keep sucking my cock. That's it, baby. Suck on it."

"Ahhhh..." Caroline moaned as she felt Mr. Lloyd's cock pressing against her asshole. She could feel her muscles stretching and she tried to relax her body as best as she could.

Mr. Lloyd pressed the head of his cock into her asshole and she cried out in pain.

"Shhh..." Andrew whispered. "Relax, baby. Relax."

Caroline closed her eyes and focused on sucking on Andrew's cock. She could feel Mr. Lloyd pushing his cock deeper and deeper into her ass.

"That's it," Andrew moaned. "Relax, darling. Relax."

"Mmm..." Caroline moaned as she felt Mr. Lloyd's cock fill her ass. She couldn't believe how full she felt. How stretched and sore. But at the same time, she also couldn't believe how good it felt.

Mr. Lloyd began to fuck her ass, slowly. "See, sweetheart? Doesn't that feel nice? Don't you feel good when you're being fucked in the ass?"

Caroline moaned as Mr. Lloyd picked up the pace, fucking her ass harder and faster. She could feel his balls slapping against her pussy with every thrust, sending jolts of pleasure and pain through her body. Her eyes were watering and she could feel wetness dripping down her chin. She knew that she must look a fright.

"Ohhh..." Mr. Lloyd groaned. "Your wife has got a tight little asshole, Andrew."

"That's right," Andrew moaned. "I love watching her take a cock up the ass."

"Mmm..." Caroline whimpered. She couldn't believe that Andrew was saying such things. She couldn't believe that she was enjoying this as much as she was. She had never felt so full in her life. She had never felt so used. So dirty.

"Ahhh..." Mr. Lloyd moaned as he fucked her harder and faster. "I'm going to come soon, Caroline."

"Mmm..." Caroline moaned as she sucked Andrew's cock. She could feel her body starting to tremble. She was close to coming, too.

"Ohhh..." Mr. Lloyd groaned as he fucked her. "Ohhh...ohhh...ahhhh!"

Caroline felt his cock pulse inside her ass and then she felt his seed explode inside her. She came hard, her whole body shaking uncontrollably as she sucked her husband's cock.

"That's it," Andrew whispered. "Keep sucking."

Caroline kept sucking, even as Mr. Lloyd pulled his cock out of her ass and stood up. He staggered over to the chair and sat down, his cock still dripping with cum.

"That was quite a show," he said, breathing heavily.

"She's a natural," Andrew agreed, his cock still in Caroline's mouth. "She'll do anything you tell her to do."

"Is that so?" Mr. Lloyd asked. "Well, then I think we should see just how far we can push her tonight. Let's take turns fucking her in every hole. Teach her everything she needs to know about being a good little wife."

"I think that's a great idea," Andrew said. "What do you think, Caroline? Want to learn how to be a good little wife for me?"

"Mmm..." Caroline moaned as she sucked Andrew's cock.

Andrew pulled Caroline off of his cock by the hair. "Turn around and face Mr. Lloyd on your hands and knees," he ordered.

Caroline did as she was told, suddenly once more ashamed now that she could see her husband's boss sitting right in front of her after what she had just allowed him to do.

"Look up at Mr. Lloyd. I want you to look him in the eye while I fuck you," Andrew ordered, lining the head of his cock up with his wife's wet pussy.

"Ohhh..." Caroline moaned as she felt her husband's cock push into her. She couldn't believe how good it felt. How full and stretched she was.

"That's it," Andrew whispered as he began to fuck her. "Look Mr. Lloyd in the eyes."

Caroline looked up at Mr. Lloyd as her husband fucked her from behind. She could see the lust in his eyes and it made her feel even dirtier. She knew that her makeup was probably smeared and her hair disheveled. But she couldn't bring herself to look away.

"Do you like the way my cock feels inside you?" Andrew asked his wife.

"Yes..." Caroline moaned as he fucked her harder.

"Do you like it when I fuck you in front of other men?"

"Yes..." Caroline whimpered as she felt her orgasm building.

"Say it," Andrew demanded. "Tell Mr. Lloyd how much you like it when I fuck you in front of other men."

"I...I..." Caroline tried to say the words but she couldn't. She couldn't believe that she was about to come in front of her husband's boss.

"Say it," Andrew demanded. "Tell him."

"I..." Caroline closed her eyes as Andrew fucked her harder. "I love it when you fuck me in front of other men."

"That's right," Andrew grunted. "You love it because you're a dirty little slut. Now come for me. Come on my cock."

"Ohhhh!" Caroline cried as she came hard, her body shaking uncontrollably as she lost control.

"That's it," Andrew whispered as he fucked her. "Keep coming. Keep coming on my cock."

Caroline moaned as she felt her orgasm wash over her. She couldn't believe how intense it was. How good it felt.

"Ohhhh!" she cried as she came again.

"That's it," Andrew whispered as he fucked her. "Keep coming. Keep coming for me."

"Mmm..." Caroline moaned again. She could feel her whole body shaking.

"Mmm..." Andrew smacked her on the ass. "Now that you've had your fun turn around so that you can take my load on your face," he ordered as he pulled his cock out of her.

"Andrew..." Caroline moaned. She couldn't believe what was happening. She couldn't believe how dirty she was feeling.

"Turn around," Andrew ordered her. "Turn around and let me come on your face."

"Ohhhh..." Caroline moaned as she turned around and faced her husband. She could see the lust in his eyes. The desire.

"That's it," Andrew whispered as he stroked his cock. "Now open your mouth. I want you to take my load on your tongue."

"Mmm..." Caroline opened her mouth and stuck her tongue out. She couldn't believe how dirty she felt. How used. How turned on.

"That's it," Andrew grunted as he came. His hot cum spurted out onto her tongue and her face and she tasted the salty, musky flavor.

"Swallow," Andrew commanded her as he jerked his cock dry.

Caroline swallowed, tasting the salty cum on her tongue. It was the first time she had ever tasted a man's seed and she found it strangely arousing.

"Good girl," Andrew whispered as he finished coming. "Now, turn around and show Mr. Lloyd how you clean up after yourself."

Caroline turned around and crawled toward Mr. Lloyd on her hands and knees. She could see the lust in his eyes as he watched her approach.

"That's right," Andrew whispered as Caroline licked his cum from the head of Mr. Lloyd's cock. "Suck him clean. Show him how much you appreciate him showing you such a good time tonight."

"Mmm..." Caroline moaned as she took Mr. Lloyd's cock in her mouth. It was already hard again and she could taste the salty tang of his seed on her tongue and she found it strangely arousing.

"That's it," Andrew whispered as he watched his wife suck Mr. Lloyd's cock clean. "You're a natural born cocksucker, Caroline. A perfect little slut. Now, suck him off and swallow every last drop of his seed."

Caroline moaned as she sucked Mr. Lloyd's cock. She could feel it growing harder as she licked and sucked him clean.

"That's it," Andrew whispered. "Keep going. You're doing such a good job."

Caroline kept sucking, licking and stroking Mr. Lloyd's cock until he came in her mouth.

"Mmm..." she moaned as she tasted his salty, musky cum on her tongue.

"Swallow," Andrew commanded her. "Swallow every last drop."

Caroline swallowed, tasting the salty, musky flavor of Mr. Lloyd's cum.

"Good girl," Andrew whispered as she swallowed. "Now, turn around and let me see your face."

Caroline turned around and looked up at Andrew. Her face was covered in cum and she felt so used and dirty. But there was also something about it that made her feel strangely aroused.

"That's right," Andrew whispered as he stared down at her. "You're a dirty little slut. A dirty little cumslut. And you love it, don't you?"

"Yes," Caroline whispered as she knelt before her husband, his cum dripping down her chin and chest. "I love it."

Andrew knelt down in front of his wife and wiped his cum from her face with his fingers. "Good girl," he said as he pushed his cum-covered fingers into her mouth.

"Well, Andrew," Mr. Lloyd was tucking himself back into his pants, "I can see that I was wrong about you. You do know how to lead. I want to see you in my office at 8 sharp Monday morning. I think we need to have a talk about your future in New York."

"Thank you, sir," Andrew said, standing up and shaking Mr. Lloyd's hand. "I'm looking forward to it."

"As am I," Mr. Lloyd nodded, smiling at Caroline who was still kneeling in front of Andrew. "And thanks for the pot roast, Mrs. Wright. Now, if you'll excuse me, I must be going. I've got a very busy day tomorrow."

"Of course," Andrew said. "I'll see you out."

Andrew walked Mr. Lloyd to the front door and Caroline remained on her knees, naked and used and feeling like a real whore. She knew that this was just the beginning of a long night of debauchery. And she couldn't wait to find out what else her husband had in store for her.

MY WIFE PAYS MY DEBTS

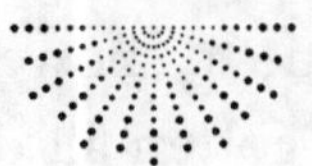

"Okay, okay. I got a good one." Ricky was drunk. He had been losing the entire night. "What's the dirtiest thing you ever got your wife to do, fellas?" He put his elbow on the table and pointed around. "Come on! I want to know!"

All of his male coworkers, friends from work, were sitting around the poker table. They all laughed, most of them had been drinking too. The topic of their wives came up earlier, and everyone took turns telling stories. It was just getting good.

"Ricky, you're a dirty fucker," said one of the men. " Why don't you tell us first? What's the dirtiest thing you ever made her do?"

Ricky shook his head and smiled. "Well, I don't know if she would like me to say." He looked at all of their faces and then grinned. "Okay, okay. I'll tell you."

"It was my birthday last year and my wife Felicia had been planning a surprise for me. I got home from work and she told me to shower and to wear something nice. She had gotten all dressed up too, and I could tell she was planning something. Scheming. When I came out of the bedroom, she was waiting for me in the living room. She had put on a sexy little cocktail dress and stockings, and she had even done her hair up in these big curls."

Ricky paused and looked at the other men. "She looked so fucking hot. She looked just like one of those pin up girls from the war back in the day when we were kids. You know, like the ones that say, 'I want a man in uniform!'"

They all laughed and nodded. They knew the type.

"So I'm asking her, 'What's going on?' And she says, 'It's your birthday! And I've got a present for you. Close your eyes!'"

"I close my eyes and then she tells me to sit down. I'm sitting on the couch. I can smell her perfume. And then, I feel her. She's right there in front of me."

Ricky looked around the room again. "Then she puts her hand on my pants. Right between my legs, on my dick. I'm getting hard already and she says, 'Do you like your present? Do you want to unwrap it?'"

The other men laughed. "Fuck yeah," said one of them. "I bet you did."

Ricky nodded. "I was so horny. I couldn't believe what she was doing. She had never done anything like this before. I just nodded my head and said yes. And then she told me to open my eyes. She stood up and lifted up her dress, and she wasn't wearing any panties!"

"I had to look twice. I was sure I was seeing things. But no, she was standing right there with her stockings on, just a garter belt, and heels. No panties. She was shaved smooth as a baby's ass! I could see her pussy lips were already wet. It was a beautiful sight."

"So then, she gets on her knees in front of me and unzips my fly. She pulls my cock out. She puts her mouth on it. She's looking up at me the whole time. It's like I'm fucking dreaming. She's sucking me off right there, with that dress still on. And guys, you know how Felicia is. She's never done anything like this before. I didn't even think she knew it was a thing girls did! I was like, 'Holy shit, she's giving me head.' And I can't believe it. My wife is blowing me on the couch! And she's so good at it. Like, she's really good at it."

Ricky paused and took a sip of his beer. He was blushing. He looked around and all of the men were looking at him expectantly.

"Come on man! Don't stop!" one of them said.

Ricky grinned. "Okay, okay. So I'm thinking to myself, 'How the hell did she get so good at this? What did she do?' I'm trying not to cum, but I'm looking at her and I can't help it. It feels so fucking good. She looks up at me and I know she's enjoying it. She's having fun. So I say to her, 'Felicia, where did you learn to do this? This is amazing.'"

"And then she takes my dick out of her mouth and looks up at me and smiles. And she says, 'I read about it in one of your magazines.' She was reading my dirty magazines! I was shocked. She kept going though. She puts my cock back in her mouth and sucks me off until I cum."

"Damn! How was she?" said another one of the men.

"Fucking amazing!" said Ricky. "And it was the best birthday present ever!"

The other men laughed and cheered.

"Fuck yeah!" one of them said.

"That's some hot stuff," said another. "I wish I could get my wife to do that. If I suggested it she'd probably drag me straight to that damn priest to get me exorcised. I can't even talk dirty to her without her getting embarrassed and telling me to shut up."

Everyone laughed.

"Yeah, well I tell ya guys, it was a shock to me. Maybe try leaving your dirty magazines lying around and your wives will get some ideas? Anyhow, who needs another beer? I'll have her get a new round. Felicia! Where are you, honey?"

"Coming!"

Everyone turned to silently watch as Felicia walked into the room with a tray of beers. She looked so innocent in her yellow dress; it was such a turn on to them to know how dirty she could really be.

"Is everything alright?" Felicia glanced around the room, noticing how the men had quieted down when she entered. "Let me bring you fellas some more food."

Felicia left to return to the kitchen, her husband and his friends watching her the whole way.

"God damn Ricky, your wife is fucking hot. You are one lucky bastard, I hope you know that," said one of the men.

"Hey, I know. And I'm gonna make her do even dirtier things tonight too, for sure. You know how it is, guys. After that blowjob she gave me, I want more. And I know how to get her to give it to me. I'm going to fuck her so good tonight. Anyhow, let's play."

Ricky started dealing the cards and everyone focused on the game again. They were all distracted by thoughts of Felicia though. They all imagined her giving them a birthday blow job like she had given her husband, and they all hoped to get another glance at her.

Ricky kept losing.

"Alright, what do I owe you now?" Ricky was losing badly.

"Another hand."

They played another hand and Ricky lost again.

"Okay, I'm out." Ricky sighed and drank from his beer. He knew he was going to be doing the dishes for a week after this. He didn't even know how much he was down and Felicia was going to be pissed. He was supposed to be saving up to take her on a vacation. He needed to win some of this money back.

"Okay, maybe one more hand. Then I'm done for the night."

They dealt the cards and everyone turned over their hands. Ricky had nothing.

"Let's make that two more hands."

Two hands turned into six and Ricky lost them all. He was down big time. He needed to win the next one or he was fucked.

"Okay, this is my last hand. If I win, you have to let me break even. Deal?"

"But what if you lose?" one of the men asked. "You already owe me like fifty bucks."

"If I lose..." Ricky looked around the room for something he could bet. "Look, if I lose I'll let you see Felicia's tits. I'll tell her to flash you."

The other men laughed and agreed. "Alright Ricky, you got a deal," said the man. "Deal the cards."

Ricky dealt the cards and looked at his hand. He was fucked.

"Alright, let's see 'em."

Everyone turned over their cards and the other men all cheered.

"Wait," Ricky panicked. "One more. And if I lose again, my wife will blow you all."

"What?" one of the guys laughed. "She's not going to do that, she's just going to kill you."

"I swear it," Ricky promised. "If I lose this last hand I'll make my wife suck you off. Just like she did on my birthday. Come on, don't you want that? It will be like your birthday. Come on, please, deal me in."

The other men laughed and thought about it. It was an amusing thought and they were all getting hard thinking about it. One of them shrugged. "Okay, Ricky. You got a deal. But if you lose this time, you better not chicken out. I'm going to collect on that."

"Deal me in."

"Okay, let's see your hand."

Ricky turned over his cards and sighed. "Fold." He didn't have anything. He knew he was fucked.

"Damn Ricky, you really lost."

"Alright, I'll call her up. Felicia! Hey, Felicia!"

Felicia came running into the room. She was wearing her yellow dress and white apron. "What is it, honey?" She looked so innocent and sweet, with her red lips and her black curls.

"Honey, would you mind coming over here for a second?"

Felicia walked over to him and Ricky put his arm around her. He had his hand on her waist. She was blushing, smiling and looking around the room at all the men.

"Honey, you see this man here?" Ricky pointed at the man who had won the hand.

"Yes, honey."

"This man here, he won the game." Ricky looked at the man and then back at Felicia. "He's a good friend of mine, and a good man. And he told me that he would really like it if you could, maybe, give him a kiss?"

Felicia's eyes went wide. She looked at the man, who was grinning and then looked back at Ricky. She blushed even more.

"Oh, honey, I don't think I can do that."

"Come on honey, it will make me happy. Can't you do this for me?" Ricky smiled at her. He knew she would do it. She always did whatever he asked her to do. "I want you to do this for me, please. It will make me so happy if you kiss my friend. Please?"

Felicia nodded and looked at the man again. He was grinning from ear to ear. She leaned over and kissed him. The man put his hand behind her neck and kissed her deeply. Felicia pulled away and stood up, blushing.

"Good girl. Thank you, honey. But that's not exactly what I meant. You see, I'm afraid that I've lost a pretty big bet, and now we owe these men. So it's either you cooperate and be a good girl, or the vacation is off."

"Ricky!" Felicia's cheeks flushed with embarrassment.

"Honey, I don't think you understand. This is serious. I lost a lot of money."

Felicia looked down and bit her lip. She looked like she was going to cry. "Okay. What do you need me to do?"

"Well, you see, these men are very horny. And I'm afraid that I lost the game. And as you know, I always keep my word. So I told them that if I lost, you would suck their dicks for them. To make up for the money I lost. They've been very good to us, Felicia. They've been very good friends to me and to this family. So, I don't think it will be a problem if you just suck their cocks, will it?"

Felicia looked at him in shock. "Ricky! How could you?"

"Get your dick out," Ricky said to the man sitting next to him. "I'll get her to work. I know she's shy. You'll see, I'll make her do it."

The man unzipped his pants and took out his cock, which was already hard after watching Felicia squirm. Ricky patted Felicia on the ass. "Go ahead, honey. Get on your knees and do it. Be a good girl. Suck his dick like I taught you."

"Ricky," Felicia whimpered.

Ricky grabbed his wife by the upper arm and pulled her down in front of the man. "Get her hair," he told the man. "Come on, Felicia," Ricky said softly. "Just open your mouth and suck his dick like you did on my birthday. Don't you want to make me happy? I know you can do it. You're such a good girl."

Felicia parted her lips and let the tip of the man's cock pass through. She licked and sucked it lightly. The man moaned in pleasure and stroked her cheek.

"See? You're doing so good." Ricky patted her on the back. "Now take him all the way in. Look how beautiful you look. All of these men want you so bad because you look so pretty right now. And you're doing such a good job. Keep going. Take him deep. You know how I like it. Come on, suck his dick nice and hard. Suck him like you would suck me."

Felicia took the man's cock all the way in her mouth and began sucking it eagerly. She was so wet. Her pussy was throbbing and aching with need. She felt so dirty and humiliated. She loved it.

The man groaned in pleasure and stroked her hair. "That's it, baby. Oh yeah. God damn. You're so fucking good at this. Keep going. Suck that cock."

The other men watched with lust in their eyes as Felicia sucked the man's cock. They were all getting hard, and they all wanted their turn.

"Come on Felicia, you can do it. Keep sucking. Look at me. You know how I like it. Look at me while you're sucking his dick. You're so fucking hot right now." Ricky stroked her hair and watched her face as she sucked the man's cock. "Do you like it? You look so good. You look so pretty. You're so beautiful. You're so good at this. Keep going. Make him cum."

Felicia moaned and sucked the man's cock hungrily.

"You like that baby? You know this would go faster if you let a few of these guys fuck you from behind while you sucked off the others. I bet you'd like that. Wouldn't you like to fuck a lot of men tonight? You look so hot right now. I can tell you want it."

Felicia moaned and sucked the man's cock, taking it in and out of her mouth. Ricky kept talking to her, telling her how sexy she was and how much he loved her. The men around her were watching with lust in their eyes, all of them wishing they could fuck her.

"Come on, Felicia. You can do it. Come on. Make him cum. Make him cum in your mouth. You're so good at this. You're such a good girl. You want another man to fuck you while you suck? Come on, let them fuck you. You know how to make a man cum."

Felicia moaned and sucked the man's cock, taking it deep into her throat. The man moaned and began to fuck her face.

"Come on, Felicia. You're so close. Just make him cum. Then you can have another man fuck you. You know you want it. You're so good at this. Come on, you can do it. Suck his dick."

Felicia sucked the man's cock and took it deep into her throat. The man groaned and began to thrust into her mouth harder and faster.

"Oh fuck. Oh fuck. Fuck yeah. That's it baby. Suck that cock. Make him cum. Make him cum down your throat. You're so fucking hot right now. You're so fucking beautiful. You look so good with a dick in your mouth. Keep going. Come on, make him cum. Make him cum in your mouth."

Felicia moaned and sucked the man's cock, taking it deep into her throat until the man couldn't hold back any longer. He came with a groan and shot his load down her throat. She swallowed it and looked up at Ricky.

Ricky smiled back at her. "Good girl. You did such a good job. Who's next? I'll let you pick this time. Which one do you want to suck?"

Felicia looked at the other men and pointed at the one sitting to her right. "That one," she said softly.

Ricky grinned at her and stroked her hair. "Such a good girl. Go on, get on your knees in front of him and suck his dick. Make him cum in your mouth. I want you to swallow all of his cum."

Felicia got on her knees in front of the man and began to suck his cock. Ricky kept talking to her, telling her how sexy she was and how much he loved her. The other men watched with lust in their eyes, all of them wishing they could fuck her.

"Hey," Ricky addressed the next man in line. "Get behind her. You see how horny she is. Just rub your dick up and down her slit a little and she'll let you put it in. She's so fucking wet. Look at her. She wants it. She's sucking that guy's dick so hard because she wants more. She's such a good littl slut. She's such a good girl. You see how she's moaning and rubbing her clit? She's so turned on. You should fuck her. Just stick your dick in her pussy. Come on, she wants it. I know she does."

The man behind Felicia put his cock up against her pussy and slowly pushed it inside of her. She was so wet and tight that he had no trouble at all entering her. She moaned around the cock in her mouth as he began to fuck her from behind.

"Come on, Felicia. Make him cum. Suck that cock. You know how I like it. Suck that cock. You look so fucking sexy right now. You're such a good girl. You're so good at this. Keep sucking. Make him cum in your mouth."

Felicia moaned and sucked the man's cock, taking it deep into her throat. The man groaned and began to thrust into her mouth harder and faster. She was so wet and tight that he couldn't hold back any longer. He came with a groan and shot his load down her throat. She swallowed it and looked up at Ricky.

"Good girl. You did such a good job. Take that dick, sweetheart. Does that feel good? You look so hot right now. You're such a good girl. You're such a good wife. You look so good getting fucked from behind like that. You should see your ass. It looks so good bouncing like that while a cock slides in and out of you. You're so fucking beautiful. You're so sexy. You're so fucking good at this. You're such a good girl. Now who's next? Who wants their dick sucked?"

Another man took the seat in front of Felicia while the one behind her continued to use her pussy. He put his cock up to her lips and she eagerly took it into her mouth. Ricky kept talking to her, telling her how sexy she was and how much he loved her. The other men watched with lust in their eyes, all of them waiting impatiently for their turn to fuck her.

"I'm about to come," the man fucking her from behind gasped. "Where do you want me to cum?"

"Come inside her pussy," Ricky said. "She's on the pill. She likes it when I shoot my load inside her. Don't you, honey? You like it when I fill up your pussy with my cum, don't you? You want all these men to come inside you? You're such a good girl. You're such a good wife. You're so fucking sexy. You're so beautiful. Come on, fill up her pussy."

The man groaned and came inside Felicia, shooting his load deep within her. She moaned and sucked the man's cock in her mouth harder, eager for more.

"That's it, Felicia. Good girl. Make him cum. Suck that cock. You know how I like it. Who wants her pussy?"

The man behind her pulled out and another man quickly took his place. He slid his cock into her pussy easily. It was so wet and slick with cum from the last man that he didn't need any lube to get in.

This man grabbed Felicia's ass cheeks as he pumped, spreading them so that he could see her tight pink asshole.

"Hey, you ever fuck her in the ass?" he asked Ricky. "I bet she'd love getting her ass fucked. You think I can slide my dick in there? I'll make her scream like a cat. Come on, let me fuck her ass. She's already wet."

Ricky nodded and looked at Felicia. "You want to let him fuck you in the ass?"

Felicia only whimpered in response. The man behind her spread her ass cheeks wide and began to work his thumb into her tight hole. Felicia struggled a little bit but the man whose cock was in her mouth helped to hold her still. He put his hand on the back of her head and began to fuck her mouth with his cock while the other man worked his thumb inside her ass.

"You like that, don't you?" Ricky said. "I know you do. You're such a naughty girl. You're such a dirty whore. You're such a slut. You're getting fucked from both ends and you love it. You're such a good girl. You're such a good wife. You're so fucking sexy. You're so beautiful. You're so fucking good at this. You're such a good girl. Come on, let him fuck your ass. If you let three men fuck you at once, think how much sooner you'll be done. Let him fuck your ass, come on. You know you want it. You're such a good girl."

The man behind her slid his thumb out and positioned his cock at her asshole. He began to press forward slowly, trying to work the tip inside her. Felicia moaned and squirmed but the two men holding her were strong and she couldn't get away.

"Come on, Felicia. It's okay. Just relax. Let him in. I know you want it. You're such a good girl. You're such a good wife. You're so fucking sexy. You're so beautiful. You're so good at this. You're such a good girl. Let him fuck your ass. Just try it. It won't hurt if you relax. You look so fucking hot right now. You're so beautiful. You're so good at this. You're such a good girl. Come on, let him in."

Felicia relaxed and the man behind her was able to slide his cock into her ass. She moaned and sucked the cock in her mouth harder. The two men fucking her began to thrust in and out of her harder and faster. Ricky kept talking to her, telling her how sexy she was and how much he loved her.

The men all groaned in pleasure as they used Felicia's body for their pleasure. They couldn't believe how lucky they Ricky was to have a wife who was such a good little slut.

"Come on, Felicia. You can do it. Make him cum. Suck that cock. You know how I like it. You're so good at this. You're such a good girl."

Felicia moaned and sucked the man's cock in her mouth harder, taking it deep into her throat. The man groaned and began to thrust into her mouth harder and faster. She was so wet and tight that he couldn't hold back any longer. He came with a groan and shot his load down her throat. She choked on it a little bit and looked up at Ricky.

"Good girl. You did such a good job. That's my girl. Who's next? One of you take her mouth and the other can have her pussy."

Another man took the seat in front of Felicia while the one behind her continued to fuck her ass. He adjusted his position so that another man was able to get underneath of her to slide into her wet cunt, which was even more tight than usual thanks to the dick up her ass.

"Oh yeah, that's it," the man underneath her groaned as he slid his cock deep within her. "Come on, Felicia. Fuck me. Ride my cock."

Felicia groaned and felt like a rag doll being fucked by all of these men at once. She felt so full and used. She was so wet and horny. She couldn't believe how much she loved being fucked like this. She had never thought of herself as a slut before, but now she couldn't believe how much she wanted it.

"Oh fuck, I'm going to come," the man fucking her ass groaned.

"Come inside her," Ricky said. "Let's fill up every hole. And only Mike is here with his dick in his hand, let him have a turn on her. Let him use her too."

The men all groaned and began to thrust in and out of Felicia harder and faster.

"Oh fuck yeah, that's it. Come on, Felicia. Take it. You like that, don't you? You're such a dirty little slut. You loved being fucked by a group of men, don't you? You were just pretending to be shy but I can tell how much you like this.

The man fucking Felicia in the ass groaned and began to shoot his load deep within her. He thrust his cock in and out of her a few times and then pulled out. Mike, the last man, quickly took his place.

The man fucking Felicia from underneath began to thrust in and out of her harder and faster. She groaned and took his cock deeper into her pussy.

"You're so beautiful," Ricky whispered to Felicia. "You're so sexy. You're such a good girl. You're such a good wife. You're doing this for us, aren't you? Think of the vacation you'll get once we pay off this debt. You're so good at this. You're such a good girl. Come on, let them cum. Make them cum. You know how to do it. You're so good at this."

Felicia moaned and began to suck the man in front of her harder and faster. The man groaned and began to thrust into her mouth. She was so wet and tight that he couldn't hold back any longer. He came with a groan and shot his load down her throat. Felicia had already swallowed so much cum that she couldn't take anymore and this man's load dripped out of her mouth and down her chin onto the man beneath her.

The man underneath of her moaned as the cum from her mouth dripped down on him. He began to thrust in and out of her pussy harder and faster until he couldn't hold back any longer. He came with a groan and shot his load deep within her. He kept thrusting his cock in and out of her until he had emptied his load completely.

Ricky watched as all of the men used Felicia for their pleasure. There was only one man left now, the one fucking her in the ass. Felicia was flushed and delirious from all the attention. Her ass was sore and stretched out but she kept getting fucked.

"Oh fuck, I'm going to come," the man fucking Felicia in the ass groaned.

"Come inside her," Ricky said. "She can take it. Let's fill her up. Come on, Felicia. Take that cock. You're so beautiful. You're such a good girl. You're doing so good."

The man fucking Felicia in the ass groaned and began to shoot his load deep within her. He thrust his cock in and out of her a few times and then pulled out.

Ricky looked at his wife, who was lying on the floor with a glazed look in her eyes. "Are you okay, honey?" he asked her gently. "Did you like that?"

Felicia nodded and smiled. "I want more," she whispered. "More cum."

Ricky grinned. "You want more cum? Well, lucky you. You still have me left. You want me to fuck you in front of all these men? You want them all to watch you take one more dick? You want to be the good little slut that you are? You want to show them what a good girl you can be?"

Felicia nodded. "Yes," she whispered. "Fuck me."

"Come on up here," Ricky pulled his dick from his pants. "Sit on this and face all these men so that they can see your face while you take this dick. Look at you, you have your makeup smeared all over and cum dripping down your chin. You're so sloppy. You're such a mess. But you look so good. You're so beautiful. You're such a good girl. Come on, sit down on this. Show these men how good you can be."

Felicia got up and straddled Ricky on the couch. She slowly lowered herself down on his cock. It slid into her easily, she was so wet and slick with cum from the other men. Her body ached but she knew that she had to finish this job. Her husband entered her from behind as a room full of men who had just taken her watched.

"Oh, honey," Ricky whispered to her. "You're all swollen. You like it when it hurts? You like it when I push my cock inside you even though your pussy is sore? I know you do. Tell me you love it. Tell me you deserve to be used by all my friends."

"I love it," Felicia moaned. "I deserve it. I want to be used by your friends. I'm a cum slut."

"Good girl," Ricky whispered. He began to thrust in and out of her hard and fast while his friends cheered him on.

"Come on, Ricky, give it to her! Make her take it! Make her take that cock!"

"Yeah, come on, Ricky! Make her take it! Make her beg for it!"

"You're such a good girl," Ricky whispered into Felicia's ear as he fucked her. "You want one more load?"

"Yes," Felicia moaned. "I want one more load."

"Good girl." Ricky began to thrust in and out of her harder and faster until he couldn't hold back any longer. He came with a groan and shot his load deep within his wife. He kept thrusting in and out of her until he had emptied his load completely.

Felicia collapsed in his arms and Ricky held her tight. He stroked her hair and kissed her on the forehead.

"Well, that's it boys," he addressed his friends. "Debt paid. See you next week?"

GET A FREE BOOK!

* * *

Be the first to find out about all of Lee Riley's new releases, book sales, and freebies by joining her VIP Mailing List. Join today and get a FREE book -- instantly!

Check Lee Riley's website spicybestsellers.com for more books.

* * *

ABOUT LEE RILEY

* * *

Lee Riley is an adventurous writer who creates spicy short stories that challenge conventions and leave readers on the edge of their seats. Drawing inspiration from their travels, Lee explores the world with insatiable curiosity, using these experiences to craft stories that captivate readers.

When not writing, Lee indulges their passion for the outdoors, discovering new culinary delights, and making connections with people from all walks of life. Their love for adventure and zest for life is reflected in their work, which is daring, unconventional, and full of surprises.

More on www.spicybestsellers.com

Contact me at lee@spicybestsellers.com

* * *

ALSO BY LEE RILEY

* * *

WIFE SHARING FANTASIES

DADDY'S NAUGHTY GIRLS

LEE RILEY
Daddy's Naughty Girls 2
DEVOURED
BY HER STEPFATHER

LEE RILEY
Daddy's Naughty Girls 3
UNDRESSED
BY HER STEPFATHER

DOMESTIC DISCIPLINE ROMANCE

LEE RILEY
6 Books!
One Price!
BACK ALLEY
DISCIPLINE
DOMESTIC DISCIPLINE
BUNDLE

LEE RILEY
5 Books!
One Price!
BACK DOOR
DISCIPLINE
DOMESTIC DISCIPLINE
BUNDLE

LEE RILEY
6 Books!
One Price!
GET PUNISHED
DOMESTIC DISCIPLINE
BUNDLE

LEE RILEY
6 Books!
One Price!
GET SPANKED
DOMESTIC DISCIPLINE
BUNDLE

HOT FFM THREESOME ACTION!

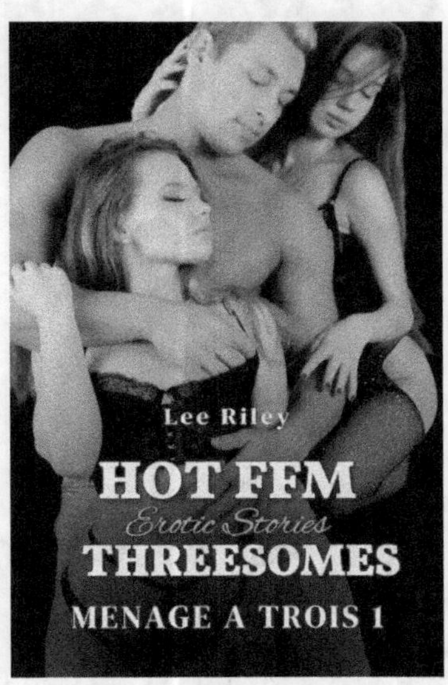

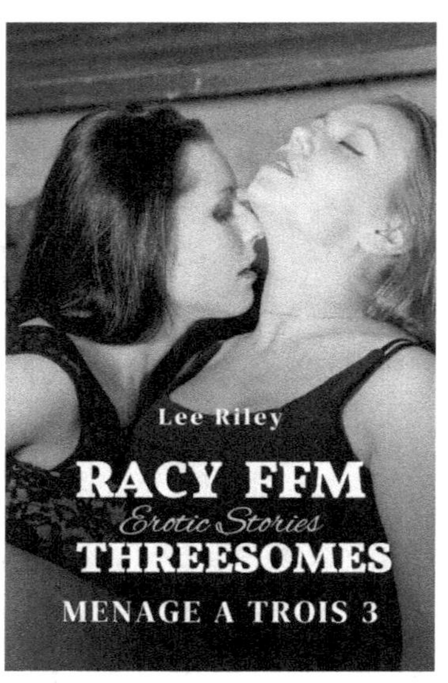

MONSTER EROTICA

LEE RILEY
MONSTROUS
ENCOUNTERS
WEREWOLVES
3 Books!
One Price!
Seductive Creatures 2

LEE RILEY
MONSTROUS
ENCOUNTERS
DEMONESSES
3 Books!
One Price!
Seductive Creatures 3

LEE RILEY
MONSTROUS ENCOUNTERS
TENTACLES & GRIM REAPER
3 Books! One Price!
Seductive Creatures 4

LEE RILEY
MONSTROUS ENCOUNTERS
KRAMPUS
Seductive Creatures 5

LEE RILEY
THE DEMON KING
LITRPG EROTICA STORIES

www.ingramcontent.com/pod-product-compliance
Lightning Source LLC
Chambersburg PA
CBHW061618130726
47996CB00003B/1032

* 9 7 9 8 8 6 9 1 8 2 3 3 3 *